PIG *the* ~~PUG~~

FIBBER

For my monkeys.

Scholastic Canada Ltd.
604 King Street West, Toronto, Ontario M5V 1E1, Canada

Scholastic Inc.
557 Broadway, New York, NY 10012, USA

Scholastic Australia Pty Limited
PO Box 579, Gosford, NSW 2250, Australia

Scholastic New Zealand Limited
Private Bag 94407, Botany, Manukau 2163, New Zealand

Scholastic Children's Books
Euston House, 24 Eversholt Street, London NW1 1DB, UK

www.scholastic.ca

The artwork in this book is acrylic (with pens and pencils) on watercolour paper.

Library and Archives Canada Cataloguing in Publication

Blabey, Aaron, author, illustrator
Pig the fibber / Aaron Blabey.
ISBN 978-1-4431-4807-8 (bound).--ISBN 978-1-4431-4808-5 (pbk.)
I. Title.
PZ10.3.B519Pf 2015   j823'.92   C2015-901880-3

Text and illustrations copyright © 2015 by Aaron Blabey.
First published by Scholastic Australia in 2015.
This edition published by Scholastic Canada Ltd. in 2015.

6 5 4 3 2 1   Printed in Malaysia 108   15 16 17 18 19

PIG the PUG FIBBER

Aaron Blabey

Scholastic Canada Ltd.
Toronto New York London Auckland Sydney
Mexico City New Delhi Hong Kong Buenos Aires

Pig was a Pug
and I'm sorry to say,
he would often tell lies
just to get his own way.

And when he would fib
he was awfully clever.
When Pig got in trouble . . .

he would always blame Trevor.

You see, he would mess up
the living room mat.

And then he'd just point and say,
"Trevor did that."

Or he'd shatter a beautiful
vase full of flowers . . .

And then he'd say,
"Trevor's been *crazy* for HOURS!"

He once even ripped up
a lovely old dress . . .

Then he hid behind Trevor
and made him confess.

"Why do you do this?"
asked poor little Trevor.

"I thought we were friends."

But Pig said, "Whatever."

Then came the day
of Pig's sneakiest plan.
He said, "I will steal
all the treats that I can!

They keep them up there,
in the closet up high.

But before I can get them,
I need a good LIE . . ."

And with that, he let fly.

It was stinky and grim.

Then he pointed at Trevor
and said, *"IT WAS HIM!"*

So Trevor was taken
outside for some air.

This was Pig's chance,
and he climbed on a chair.

"Those treats will be mine!
And *I'LL*
GOBBLE
THEM ALL!"

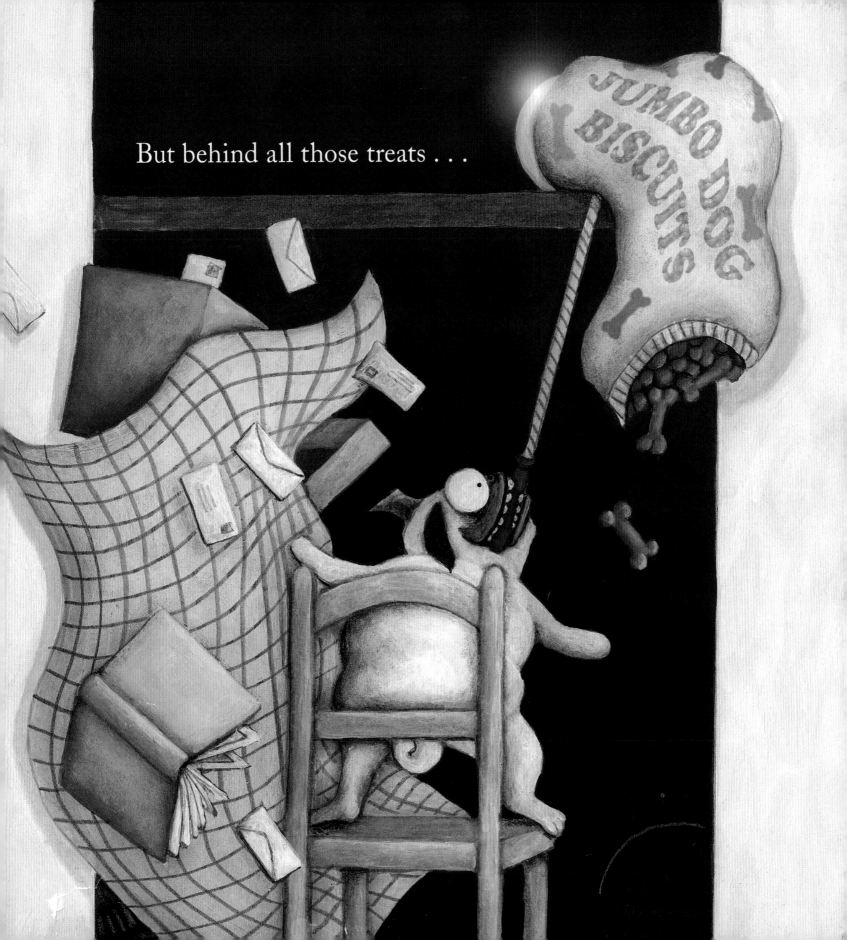

But behind all those treats . . .

. . . was an old bowling ball.

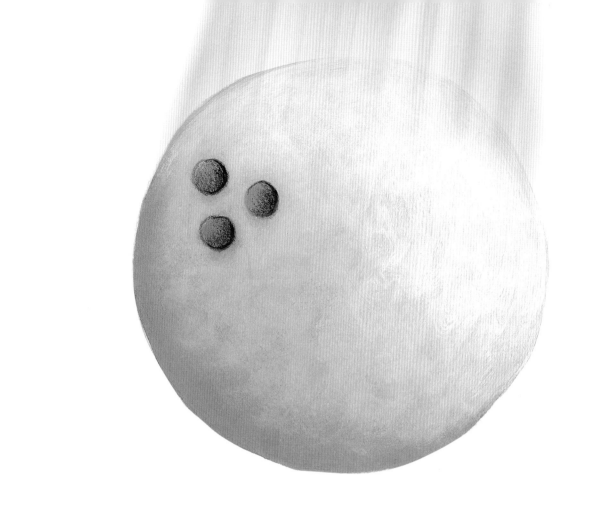
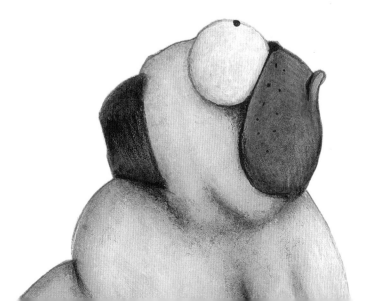

These days it's different,
I'm happy to say.
Pig has stopped lying!
Hip hip hooray!

He may have some bruises.
And one less front tooth.
But he sure learned his lesson . . .

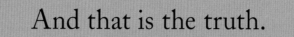

And that is the truth.

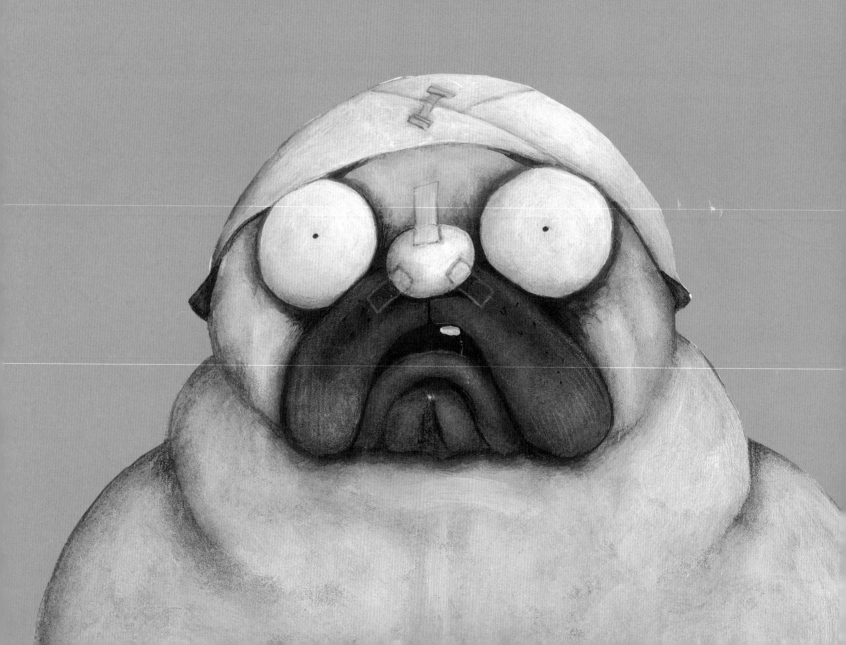